Favorite Stories from

Cowgirl Kate and Cocoa

Horse in the House

Favorite Stories from Cowgirl Kate and Cocoa

Horse in the House

Written by **Erica Silverman**

Painted by **Betsy Lewin**

Green Light Readers
Houghton Mifflin Harcourt
Boston   New York

To Ralph, in loving memory —E. S.
To Erica —B. L.

Text copyright © 2009 by Erica Silverman
Illustrations copyright © 2009 by Betsy Lewin

First Green Light Readers edition, 2018

For information about permission to reproduce selections from this book, write to trade.permissions@hmhco.com or to Permissions, Houghton Mifflin Harcourt Publishing Company, 3 Park Avenue, 19th Floor, New York, New York 10016.

hmhco.com

The text type was set in Filosofia.
The display type was hand-lettered by Georgia Deaver.
The illustrations in this book were done in watercolors on Strathmore one-ply Bristol paper.

The Library of Congress has cataloged *Cowgirl Kate and Cocoa: Horse in the House* as follows:
Silverman, Erica.
Cowgirl Kate and Cocoa: horse in the house/written by Erica Silverman; painted by Betsy Lewin.
p. cm.
ISBN 978-0-15-205390-1 hardcover
ISBN 978-0-547-31672-7 paperback
Summary: When Cocoa decides to explore the house, Cowgirl Kate has a hard time convincing him he must return to the barn.
[1. Horses—Fiction. 2. Cowgirls—Fiction. 3. Dwellings—Fiction.] I. Lewin, Betsy, ill. II. Title.
PZ7.S58625Cof 2009
[E]—dc22 2007043356

ISBN: 978-1-328-89580-6 GLR paperback
ISBN: 978-1-328-90089-0 GLR paper over board

Manufactured in China
SCP 10 9 8 7 6 5 4 3 2 1

4500697916

A Small Stall

Cowgirl Kate felt horse whiskers on her face.

She woke up.

She opened her eyes.

"Cocoa!" she said.

"How did you get into the house?"

Cocoa grinned.

"I pushed the door open
and walked in," he said.

"You have to leave!" cried Cowgirl Kate.

"What if my parents see you?"

"They won't," said Cocoa.

"I saw them drive off in the truck."

"They'll be back," said Cowgirl Kate.

She jumped out of bed.

She got dressed.

"Come on," she said.

"I'll walk you back to the barn."

"I'm tired of the barn," said Cocoa.

"And I've always wanted to explore

the house."

He looked under the bed.

"Where's your hay?" he asked.

"Cocoa," said Cowgirl Kate,

"you have looked in my window many times.

Have you ever seen any hay?"

"I thought you were hiding it," said Cocoa.

He sniffed the rug.

He looked behind the dresser.

Then he snorted.

"No hay!

What kind of stall *is* this?"

"It's a bedroom," said Cowgirl Kate.

"People sleep in bedrooms.

Horses belong in barns."

"I belong with you," said Cocoa.

"But your stall is too small."

He turned and walked out.

"Where are you going?" asked Cowgirl Kate.

"To find a bigger stall," said Cocoa.

The Best Stall of All

"I will give you a snack," said Cowgirl Kate.

"I would like a snack," said Cocoa.

"But then," said Cowgirl Kate,

"you must promise to go back to the barn."

"Do I have to?" asked Cocoa.

Cowgirl Kate nodded. "Promise?"

"I promise," said Cocoa.

"Okay, follow me," said Cowgirl Kate.

Cowgirl Kate led Cocoa into the kitchen.

She opened the refrigerator door.

"Yeehaw!" cried Cocoa. "A giant bin.

And it's filled with food."

"It's called a refrigerator,"

said Cowgirl Kate.

"Refrigerator," Cocoa repeated.

He gazed at all the food.

He smacked his lips.

"Do you want an apple or a carrot?"
asked Cowgirl Kate.

"Yes, please," said Cocoa.

Cowgirl Kate smiled.

She gave him an apple and a carrot.

Then she gave him another apple and
another carrot.

"This is the best stall in the house!"
said Cocoa.
"This is where I will live!"

Cowgirl Kate shook her head.

"You must leave now," she said.

"My parents will be home soon."

"But I don't want to leave," said Cocoa.

"But you promised," said Cowgirl Kate.

"But I love the house," said Cocoa.

"Well, I love the barn," said Cowgirl Kate.

Cocoa snorted.

"What's so great about the barn?" he asked.

"Come on," said Cowgirl Kate.

"I will show you."

Cocoa took one last look around the kitchen.

He nuzzled the refrigerator.

He sighed.

"Cocoa, hurry!" said Cowgirl Kate.

"My parents are coming!"

Cowgirl Kate led Cocoa to the barn.

"It's just a barn," said Cocoa.

"What is there to love?"

Cowgirl Kate pointed.

"I love how the sunlight comes in
through the cracks in the wall," she said.

Cocoa looked.

"That is nice," he said.

Cowgirl Kate inhaled deeply.

"And I love the smell of saddle leather and fresh hay," she said.

Cocoa sniffed.

"That is a good smell," he said.

"And I love
   the sound of all the horses
   snorting and stomping, nickering
   and neighing," said Cowgirl Kate.
Cocoa perked up his ears.
"Me, too," he agreed.

Cowgirl Kate stroked Cocoa's neck.

"But what I love best about the barn,"
she said, "is you."

Cocoa thought for a moment.

Then he said, "It's true. The barn would
not be the same without me."

"Exactly!" said Cowgirl Kate.

"Okay. I will live in the barn," said Cocoa.

"But I will visit the house, too."

Cowgirl Kate sighed.

"Do you have to?" she asked.

"Yes," said Cocoa.

"The barn is my home, but there are two

things in the house that I love."

"What are they?" asked Cowgirl Kate.

"You," said Cocoa.

"And the refrigerator."